This striking collection of poems is a compelling fusion of contrasting energies. It is at once meditative, lyrical and deeply political. But that's the poet Lucy Holme for you, she's a writer with a rare gift for holding impossible tensions and singing them into lucid, invaluable poems. *Temporary Stasis* is a haunting exploration of the feminine and the marine; woman and ocean mix and merge as Lucy Holme's potent lines dive us toward a profound understanding of the acquamarine, and the powers and vulnerabilities of the feminine.

— Grace Wells, *The Church of the Love of the World*


Lucy Holme's *Temporary Stasis* has the potential of a moment when something is about to happen: some unleashing, or some potential wild rebellion. In a chapbook made up of short, vivid sequences, the stories of women are foregrounded, especially how girls and women are conditioned to be small, to take up little space, to serve, but the water that flows through many of these poems, the all-encompassing seas, offer other possibilities to the narrators. Some scenarios are disturbingly familiar, like poems that document the framing of women as mere objects to service some men. The book laments the banal limits of macho fantasy in poems like 'Secret Closet'. Other poems contemplate women's lives from the view of an older woman, like the speaker in 'Lane Swimming in the Club Natació' who refuses to work out to get in shape but instead "to tally the years, with a heart made stronger". Altogether, this collection offers an intriguing assortment of poems which critique the narrowness of roles set forth for girls. There is hope too however, as inspired by closeness with nature and especially water, older narrators remain on a quest for more nourishing and sensuous possibilities.

— Zoë Brigley, *Hand & Skull*

# TEMPORARY STASIS

*Lucy Holme*

© 2022 Lucy Holme. All rights reserved; no part of this book may be reproduced by any means without the publisher's permission.

ISBN: 978-1-915079-36-7

The author has asserted their right to be identified as the author of this Work in accordance with the Copyright, Designs and Patents Act 1988

Cover designed by Aaron Kent

Edited and typeset by Aaron Kent

Broken Sleep Books Ltd
Rhydwen,
Talgarreg,
SA44 4HB
Wales

# *Contents*

### **TERRA FIRMA**
| | |
|---|---|
| a girl | 10 |
| Pruning for Beginners | 11 |
| Working Titles for this Poem Include... | 13 |

### **OCEAN-GOING**
| | |
|---|---|
| Flying Fish | 16 |
| first day nerves | 17 |
| Late Shift | 18 |
| Housekeeping | 19 |

### **THALASSIC**
| | |
|---|---|
| appliqué | 22 |
| Submerge | 23 |
| The next bar | 24 |
| Secret Closet | 26 |

### **ADRIFT**
| | |
|---|---|
| pierce here | 28 |
| Temporary Stasis | 29 |
| Cities from the Sea | 31 |
| Wilderness | 34 |

### **AFLOAT**
| | |
|---|---|
| Lane Swimming in the Club Natació | 38 |
| Lighting the Wreck | 40 |
| The Lament of a Future Daughter of Neptune | 41 |

| | |
|---|---|
| Acknowledgements | 43 |

# Temporary Stasis

Lucy Holme

This book is written in memory of Colin Holme (1933-2019).
*He would have loved to have seen the whole picture.*

# Terra Firma

Doctor:

What are you doing here, honey? You're not even old enough to know how bad life gets.

Cecilia:

Obviously, Doctor, you've never been a 13-year-old girl.

— from *The Virgin Suicides*, Jeffrey Eugenides

## *a girl*

— from *Loose Covers for Easy Chairs* in *Hundreds of Things a Girl Can Make*, W. Foulsham & Co., Ltd

When attached satisfactorily,
hem a way to the shade.
A row of stitches. A slot.

Narrow thread. A bod.
A small frill; keep free,
finish light.

Slip up, gather tight.
The end cannot be seen.
Carefully conceal as much as possible;

low, little bulb.

Bright colours, look attractive —
stiff underneath.

Act kind, sufficient. Give support.
Loose, easy.

Submit to
the average.

## *Pruning for Beginners*

> All that I love
> I fold over once
> And once again
> And keep in a box.
> — from *Bonsai*, Edith Tiempo

My first boyfriend had a bonsai tree.
Used dainty secateurs to tend her glossy leaves.

I read the book his mother gave him
on the ancient art, underlined points
in the chapter on fertilisation,

on allowing sufficient room
for her roots to spread and grow.

We made love on the bathmat of his en-suite.
Under the Velux he left ajar on sticky June nights.

And as I fixed upon her tiny canopy,
the pillow folded underneath my head —

I recall his heat rash and the lack of space;
the impossibly narrow confines of her plot —

the fear she might starve to death
in that modern bungalow, in the suburbs.
Pinned into a rigid cage, ambition dwarfed.

Though we had blossomed under heated glass,
I sought new rituals to learn.
Knew soon I would outgrow my past.

We played Jenga as the summer rain
fell jagged on the roof, and I removed
each wooden brick, piece by piece.

Does she live? I'd like to know. Majestic, gnarled,
moulded by expert fingers. Unruly stems
curtailed by a careful, steady clipping.

I still dream the outline of her limbs.
Her twisted ornamental branch.
The shadow she cast across his bedroom wall.

## *Working Titles for this Poem Include...*

*brown school skirt* in honour of those stiff and unforgiving pleats.
How they buckle and warp when the waistband
is rolled.
You walk from school, through town, past the prison, home,
imagining what life will be like
when you are older.

*Castles for Cosette* and *Tunnels for Eponine*,
distant gunfire over a papier mâché
motte-and-bailey castle you made at junior school.
It is a skill to build defenses against scalding oil cauldrons and quicklime;
to mould cotton-wool sheep and pipe cleaner battering rams.

A castle is a room in which to hoard
ambitions,
where you pack relics into tea chests, along with expectations.
Later, you yearn for *lost sketches* of moon faces
and tiny triangle bodies,
of that house you loved, a box with a chimney,
an accident of birth in felt-tips.

*Much too soon* for the Greek waiter you met in Rhodes at fifteen.
*Far too old* for the DJ who pushed your head
into his lap in a lane.

It is your *part-time job* at the Stakis, and a scum-filled bucket of
cutlery to polish
at the bronze package hotel where dreams discolour and tarnish.

*Cycling at speed*, anorak flapping,
gum wound around your tongue, standing

outside Benetton at eleven in your knee-
high boots,
with your *childhood like a siren* screaming *wait!*
*Not so fast*,
as you lean against the milkshake splattered telephone booth.

No, you don't worry about time or loss on that walk home from school,
that today might be *the last day your mum*
*picks out your clothes.*
So confident you'll never want for more or leave.
Your *idyllic, painful, naïve teenage years.*

# Ocean – going

Are you alive?
I touch you.
You quiver like a sea-fish.
I cover you with my net.
What are you — banded one?
— *The Pool*, H.D

## Flying Fish

Atoms condense, fluid flows free
stubborn ocean weight compresses all.
Overhead, the skyline sprawls. Violet clouds
like mackerel scales scattered on glass,
suspended over blinking white-capped waves.

A flying fish swoops in a quivering arc
and with a thick *thud*, skittles across the deck.
She comes to rest near the scuppers —
a shining scintilla of hope that you might yet
fathom this wide and sweeping sea.

You kneel, watch her fin-wings beat a sombre tune,
see the slate grey forked tail's flicker.
A slick torpedo hurled from the blue depths
took flight for a glorious second
then crashed.

Photo by Charlotte Saunders

## *first day nerves*
*— from A Traveller's Washing Compendium in Hundreds of Things
a Girl Can Make,* W. Foulsham & Co., Ltd

One becomes dirty so quickly,
the feeling of comfort washed away,

      the requisites of a small space.

A miniature cake of soap, a face-glove,
a pocket-comb, a tiny mirror —

items are arranged as follows:
fold, strip, roll up, take up

      very little space

but, naturally,
it is a choice.

A piece of glazed cloth, thin,
supple, waterproof.

Do you recognise yourself?

      U r waterproof —

but, be careful.

## *Late Shift*

Today may be the day I make it through.
By that, I mean, survive a dinner service
Without him stroking the back of my arm
Every chance he gets.

A can of *Diet Coke*, my trusted friend, stands,
Half-filled with vodka.
Waits for the swish of the pantry door,
My return from the main salon.

Used to be I'd sneak one
After all was clean and stowed.
Guests in bed, coast clear.

I'd lay on the bow in tuxedo trousers and shirt.
Cross tie unclipped, suit jacket ditched.
I'd count stars and feel lucky.

Now it's earlier. Five o'clock, fresh
From break — to take off the edge.
Make it easier to feign strength.

And if my colour is up and tongue loose,
Tonight may be the night
I ask him not to touch me again.

Or perhaps I will tidy the aft, hide away.
Until this shift is finished.

## *Housekeeping*

Sure, I can bring your coffee, Sir.
Clean your cabin, change the sheets.
It's not for us to uncover squalid bilge water,
or disturb the slithering beasts.
So, I'll turn my head to avoid porn scenes playing.
Gather rigid tissues from your waste basket.
Convince you I am qualified.

I am qualified.

One summer, twice a day, I emptied condoms
from an Alpine chalet bin whose owners
(Christian ramblers) never spoke a word
to each other at breakfast.

The team nicknamed me *jism hand* —
though I always wore a rubber glove.
I didn't mind; I liked the job.

There have been many/incalculable/inestimable
bodily fluids spilled since.
A litany of stains which are at first glance
impervious to treatment.
But armed with a Dr Beckmann stain devil
we are nothing if not persistent.

Will my curriculum vitae be complete
with this new opportunity?
The *vitae*, the course of my life
has run haphazardly in this industry
with value according only to how you view me.

And I will never be told the ways
in which I didn't measure up.
But I should take notes, remember the rules
or I will never make the grade.

I am qualified

but I have yet to hit the big time,
tired, subdued, nearly out of breath.
I started halfway up and hoped to climb,
to be the best. Closed my eyes
to subjugation, so I wouldn't see
what's happening on this yacht —
where interior crew are girls
and girls are handy to have around.

But not essential, not *professional*.
Never qualified.
We are expendable, elastic.

Flexible as latex.

# Thalassic

Apparently
peripatetic, it pops up

wherever I go, glistening
on my shoulder, a gold epaulette,

a stuffed piñata
albatross of bubble-gum, filter tips,

and lottery tickets, glossy
cascades of laminated sleaze

difficult to care about,
much harder to reject.
> — from *Trimmings*, Frances Leviston

## *appliqué*
> — from *French Knots and Couching* in *Hundreds of Things a Girl Can Make,* W. Foulsham & Co., Ltd

Maybe the point is not
to *push through,* to hold firm,
but — to slip the knot.

Desire, space — two kinds of need;
one fine and one coarse,
must be the outline.

We thread through the dawn,
make a stitch, inch further along
and continue — as ornaments.

The addition of a touch to the neck
and wrists, is useful

in embroidery.

## *Submerge*

She contemplates a mourning sea,
set alight with algae, sprinkled with smooth,
broad swimmers' shoulders.
Rhythmic treading, chestnut bodies four feet
from the beach gauge the day's impending
toil and heat.
In front, a line of *medusae* guard the shingle strip
take watery sentry posts at daybreak,
link tentacles to form a wave attenuating fence.
She glides past those who have not missed
this daily ritual in seventy summers
and with fresh welts turns to survey
the shore. Unlike a jellyfish, she has a brain
but doubts her instinct for survival
  *swoop siren, dive under.*
She is touched by mysterious creatures, half-a-billion
years old, her neat square of belongings,
a tear on the rocks,
as she joins the choral bobbing.
With skin salt-crisped, hair in ropes
a spark of gelatinous energy jolts her from reverie.
She returns to the sand, examines the keloid fan-lashes,
smokes cigarettes on worn, striped chairs
  *swim now, fix later*
goes back to primitive fantasies of breaking
barriers, of changing the tide.
The livid purple scars stay for a week, then fade.
Cells absorbed. She never swims in a dawn ocean again.

## *The next bar*

We start early at Orient Bay, towels
on loungers by twelve, lunch at two.
Order *Domaines Ott* and *Salades de Crevettes*
with pale green palm hearts,
a salt crusted *baccalao* for main.

Play at being connoisseurs, foodies.
Like charter guests. We click fingers
at waiters, guzzle frozen daiquiris,
stress that our steaks should be
*medium rare.*

By three we are inserting whole wine glasses
into our mouths, plates pushed away.
Sense long since departed.

We tell jokes with no discernible punchline
smoke menthols, fall backwards
off wicker chairs into the sand,

jump unbidden into the sea,
and hope that our boutique tie-dyed
sarongs don't weigh us down.

We gawp at nudists walking
the glassy beach as if we have never seen
naked, free-hanging bodies before.

By five, table cleared of broken shellfish
and ashtrays and empty bread-baskets
we are planning the next assault,
the next round of sickly shots.

In the minivan, the driver looks patiently ahead,
as Britney Spears's *Everytime* plays
and we bellow louder, LOUDER!
And lean our sunburned heads
against the windows.

As we pass Grand Case at nine,
some of us cry, missing home.
Not yet knowing who the hell we are.
Or what we are doing here.

We are all just waiting for the second wind
to pick us up and take us onward.
To the next bar.

## Secret Closet

His closet was not a place in which he kept much of anything at all. Apart from a tripod with a camera perched on top, there were shelves. Empty, gleaming and spotless shelves which did not contain clothes or possessions and which we regularly cleaned even though this was a private place, which we were not supposed to access with our Miele nozzles, cotton buds and microfibre cloths. But even private places have to be kept clean. This closet had a double purpose. A mirror within a wardrobe. It was a badly kept secret. Every day we would press the place on the mirror that opened the door and step inside to check what fresh additions had been made to the costumes hanging on the dress-up bar, a bronze rail from which hung a couple of jewelled cocktail gowns, négligée with feathered trim, a latex nurse's uniform, and a playboy bunny girl leotard with a fluffy tail. All bore the tidemarks of various shades of foundation and bronzer, all were fragranced with a heady concoction of myriad summer edition perfumes. Underneath were several pairs of zip-up kinky boots and packets of fishnet stockings and suspenders. Nothing particularly dark, deviant or very imaginative. Regular, ordinary fantasy outfits for use with regular, ordinary fantasies. The clothes were *one size fits all*. The women were *one size fits all*. We never saw a woman onboard who could not fit into the clothes from the secret closet. We never saw a woman bring any clothes onto the boat in their own luggage. We never saw the same woman more than once, except for his girlfriend, who it seemed was unaware of the existence of the secret closet. As we tidied the master cabin daily, Angela would take a Viagra from the porcelain dish next to the bed. 'What? He doesn't count them,' she would argue. 'He won't miss one.' She'd just pop it into her mouth like a tic-tac as she stripped and re-made monogrammed duvet covers and ironed top sheets. On guest drop-off days we left the secret closet until last, to clean and organise. After we had waved off the final guests, and the limousine tender disappeared around the headland, one of us would then take a pair of boots and put them on with our white formal shorts and webbed belt, and come strutting out of the Master Cabin down the side deck to fling a leg up onto a service station and do some approximation of a striptease. We always jumped into the water in our uniforms once we received confirmation that the guests were out of sight, removing the boots before we climbed the capping rail, and let go.

# ADRIFT

Rocking on the crest
In the low blue lustre
Are the shadows of the ships
       — from *Sketch*, Carl Sandburg

## *pierce here*
— from *Posies Made of Beech-Masts in Hundreds of Things a Girl Can Make*, W. Foulsham & Co., Ltd

At the end of time, bind
with strips.

Cling to beech-masts,
make the posies even
make the posies roar,
as you please.

If you care, brush gold.
Paint over a few.
They will look smart
bound up.

But a whole posy of gilt
seldom looks neat.

## *Temporary Stasis*

> But more than the many-foamed ways
> Of the sea,
> I know him
> — *Hermes of the Ways*, H.D

# I

I grab the lighter from my red beach bag.
Inside are grains of sand
and dusky pink shells,
used train-tickets to coastal towns

the hidden kind with rocky coves,
a *passagiate* and striped parasols,
in neat yellow rectangular
rows.

My leather sandals chafe from the walk,
wings clipped for now.
Head heavy, eyelids raw.

Windblown pines on the Cinque Terre
release trails of marching ants.
They mimic my mind,
which doesn't rest.

Home and familiarity beckon.
But I — halfway through this tempestuous voyage,
and interrupted by foul weather —
resist predictability.

Behind lenses tinted dark,
alone at a travertine table.
I take a hit of treacled espresso
ripened by this sweet Italian heat.

## II

Storms of winter long since passed,
I welcome the season's demise.
The chance to stay here forever
under cloudless blue.

To stay, take root.
Remain for a person, a place,
a shingle beach.

But familiar faces warp in the haze,
between now and then,
as the white capped waves retract
to welcome me back in.

Brow slick, as nicotine
and August's memories
meld,

I ruminate on those early
guileless, wandering days
and taste the last few exquisite rays.

## *Cities from the Sea*

I pedal fast on Syndicato, the concrete
hard, under my bicycle's frame.

The girls on Carrer de la Justicia
cackle in crochet bras and hotpants,
feet weary from a busy shift,
cracked soles caked with street dust,
they holler to neighbours in the Plaça Quartera.

When I walk in Parc de la Mar,
in Joan Miro's careful footsteps,
I look back out to the ocean,
a hesitant, unpractised wayfarer;

the years spent peering at cities
from the sea, from the breakwater.
Dazzled by a circuit board of tiny lights
blinking at night.

Through binoculars I see
no pleasure cruisers, but — rubber boats
in peril, vessels in distress.
Human cargo with capsized dreams.

The faint light of their mobile phones,
their weak cries for help.
*Menors extranjero no acompañado,*

so-called *aliens* — like me, unlike me.
Spurred on by hope, by the dream
of a new, safer city to make their own.

I will miss the mornings, awake at dawn
to count the coils of the anchor chain
as it huffed to the ocean floor,

with every jetty came the same promise;
two feet on dry land in San Juan,
Virgin Gorda, Palma de Mallorca,
to disappear into narrow lanes,
into the clatter of pavement cafes.

When language left me guttural,
I would meet the eyes of strangers,
tread velvet algae paths
to sea-scented wisteria gardens.

Spend hours on a mahogany tan
to complement my shiny passport —
stored, stamped and safe
inside a leather briefcase.

Spend years raising ensigns at dawn
only to lower them at dusk.
Legitimised by flags.

Though often blinded
by the pilot boat's bright lights,
I still hear their voices, mourn their plight
and recognise the ease
with which I travelled the world,

in those cities that I made my own.

## *Wilderness*

After lengths of coastline marked
by dust and roots,
sand stretched to water's edge,

stood Cocos Keeling's glinting atoll.
The only haven for vagrant birds
blown south.

We kept a desolate tract,
1940.2 nautical miles
from the Maldives;

dropped anchor at Direction island
at the tail end of the Doldrums.
I felt sure there was a tempest brewing,

but I must remember wrong.
The season called for sanctity,
spoke of stillness and of calm.

We snorkelled the rip
with humphead wrasse,
dived shallow shipwreck graves.

That day, I caught my flesh
on ruthless coral and it frayed.
Blood glowed green under refracted rays

while red hermit crabs in endless undulations,
rolled past, to the shores
of the Indian Ocean.

Escapees from earthen burrow homes,
guided by a waning moon,
by ancient tides.

I stepped across their frantic river,
my soft feet unprepared
for cuttlefish sharp soil.

I see them now;
horn-eyed, ghostly crabs
squatting low.

I hear the clacking hum.
Their fragile sacs gathered
close to abdomen.

In a rush, they released
a thousand sticky orbs,
streamed to lava into the surf.

Then, dancing, wild and untamed —
red mothers, maybe
even drowning

that their own should live,
shook off the rabid frenzy
of birth and imminent death.

I did not understand their dance;
I had my own clean,
orchestrated moves.

And as the seamount rose,
I did not recognise
the honour in their furtive race.

Unaware that in later years,
a million miles from Cossies beach,
I would beg doctors to slice me open,

to take her out, rather
than I go on without her.
That I would scuttle back from myself,

from my pulsating frame,
desperate to deposit my sac
safely on the shore.

I did not know back then
that tidal waves return the buried
hulls of sunken ships —

compositor wrecks, ribs extended,
swollen with the brine.
That I too would be set adrift.

That at the end of your life
when the storms have died down
you might ask *what exactly did I risk?*

# AFLOAT

And kneeling at the edge of the transparent sea I shall shape for myself a new heart from salt and mud.
— from *Tango XXIV, The Beauty of the Husband,* Anne Carson

## *Lane Swimming in the Club Natació*

I go to Son Hugo to count lengths
and exercise regret with a forward crawl.
To let grief fade — an aural rush, then the silent
contemplation which pervades. Yet even adding
numbers proves too hard; my shaky maths aside,
I don't know when it all went wrong.

*Concentrate. Do I calculate breaths or list mistakes?*

Was it five or seven years? Less, with absence added?
Funny how you only see a fraction of the whole.
Yes, that's right — the date swims into view —
five years married, two since I had begun
to prefer the single digit known as one.
I subtract to twenty-three, peer at life numerically.

*The benefits of backstroke are a heightened sense of self control
and, of course, a tightened core.*

Twenty-four. Twenty-four equals Panama,
my feet burnt raw from the Islas San Blas,
hot white sand trickles through tanned fingers.
At the fair in Mission Beach, at twenty-five
we held hands on a fluoro ferris-wheel.
Never thought one day, that we'd divide.

*I overtake old Spanish ladies, their silvery hair combed
high and dry*

I watch myself on the stern of a sleek modern ketch.
Bold and audacious with arms outstretched.

I was twenty-six when we sailed the Haro strait.
Currents lethal, but for the following wind.
Near Vancouver Island I spy the four yellow salt-
hills, sunlight floods the rafters and I try to keep pace.

*Take a breath, it's okay, the memory will fade.*

Through the iron girders in the gabled roof, I see sky.
I'm twenty-seven, Vermentino in my glass,
dressed in an orange sundress you said you liked.
Thirty. That summer — in Nice's Cours Saleya
market — I found a portrait, took it home.
Called her *girl in blue*. She looked like me.

*I float and I do not sink.*

The numbers climb. Thirty-two, to thirty four.
I multiply, add hope. A new formula appears.
Each stroke brings further clarity, less fear.
These days I no longer work out to sculpt my
shoulders or shear my thickening waistline —
but to tally the years, with a heart made stronger.

*Adjust the incremental gains, measure strides made by me alone.*

## *Lighting the Wreck*

A single flare launched
over dun November seas —
illuminates all

## *The Lament of a Future Daughter of Neptune*

A day away from slimy induction
by the King and his helper.

Across the Equator's watery line,
they catch a fish.

We stand transfixed as the silver light
swoops and sways on its cord
through the waves.

Then — hoisted and hooked,
bashed and sliced, blood sprayed
into scuppers,

all remains cleaned
from sun-bleached decks —
they hold her up.

We smile, recoil.
Peer into one unblinking eye.
Register nothing.

Just a baby, they say,
as they gather their tools
and begin their work.

## *Acknowledgements*

To Jenny Holme, for being my earliest and most encouraging reader and to Garry Roberts, and Este, Tuilelaith and Felix Holme-Roberts, for the love, familial support and endless distraction.

Poems in this collection have been previously featured (in sometimes slightly different forms) in the following publications: *An Capall Dorcha, Beir Bua, Ekphrasis Magazine, Indelible Literary Journal, The Liminal Review, Poetry Birmingham* and *Porridge Literary Magazine*.

The poems, A Girl, Pierce Here, First Day Nerves and Appliqué are erasures I made from the book *Hundreds of Things a Girl Can Make* first published by W. Foulsham & Co., Ltd in 1900.

Thanks go to Brian Lynch for shortlisting poems from this pamphlet for the Patrick Kavanagh Award 2021 and also to the Munster Literature Centre for a mentoring fellowship. Thanks, in particular, to Grace Wells, without whom these poems, together in a collection, would not exist. Thank you for pushing me slowly towards the truth and for helping me to rediscover the depth of love I had for the ocean after all.

To Aaron Kent and Charlie Baylis, thank you for noticing my work, for being visionary publishers and for creating such a vibrant, inclusive and diverse press as Broken Sleep Books. I am honoured to be part of this movement. To Naush Sabah, thank you for being a creative inspiration, an exceptional editor and font of knowledge. To Zoë Brigley, my thanks for reading the poems so closely and for understanding what I had hoped to convey.

Thanks also to the members of The Poetry Society Irish Stanza group, Cheltenham Poetry Festival, Ó Bhéal, iamb, and to Joanna Walsh and the Write With study group. I am grateful to the following poets, writers and friends who have all contributed with help, suggestions, confidences or feedback such as Wendy Allen, Sara Angelica Axelsson, Sarah Byrne, Paul Casey, Nicola Jones, Roula-Maria Dib, Damien Donnelly, Laura Hannay, James Harris, Taidgh Lynch, Stuart McPherson, Mary Ford Neal, Liz Quirke, Kali Richmond, Julia Gomes Rodon, Charlotte Saunders, Mindy Simpson, Victoria Summers, Lucy Sunnucks, Emma Timmins, Maria Tracey, and James Wilson.

# LAY OUT YOUR UNREST

CPSIA information can be obtained
at www.ICGtesting.com
Printed in the USA
BVHW011107200822
645022BV00021B/134

9 781915 079367